Sona and the Wedding Game

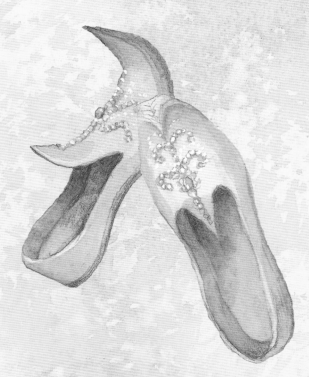

Written by
Kashmira Sheth

Illustrated by
Yoshiko Jaeggi

Ω
PEACHTREE
ATLANTA

Published by
PEACHTREE PUBLISHERS
1700 Chattahoochee Avenue
Atlanta, Georgia 30318-2112
www.peachtree-online.com

Text © 2015 by Kashmira Sheth
Illustrations © 2015 by Yoshiko Jaeggi

Book design and composition by Loraine M. Joyner
Decorative borders created by Christine Dengel Baum

The illustrations were rendered in watercolor on 100% rag
archival watercolor paper. The title was created using
Microsoft Corporation's Harrington by Sam Wang; text is
typeset in Linotype Corporation's Sabon by Jan Tschichold.

Printed in November 2014 by Tien Wah Press in Malaysia
10 9 8 7 6 5 4 3 2 1
First Edition

Library of Congress Cataloging-in-Publication Data

Sheth, Kashmira.
   Sona and the wedding game / by Kashmira Sheth ;
illustrations Yoshiko Jaeggi.
      pages cm
   ISBN 978-1-56145-735-9
   Summary: Sona is excited about attending her first Indian
wedding, especially since her sister is the bride, but when she
learns that tradition requires her to steal the groom's shoes
during the ceremony she must ask her annoying little cousin,
Vishal, for help.
 [1. Weddings—Fiction. 2. East Indian Americans—Social life
and customs—Fiction. 3. Brothers and sisters—Fiction. 4.
Family life—Fiction.] I. Jaeggi, Yoshiko, illustrator. II. Title.
   PZ7.S5543
   [Sil 2015]
   [E]—dc23
                       2014006501

For Rupa and Joey
—*K. S.*

For Dan and Aditi
—Y. J.

MY GRANDPARENTS AND MY COUSIN
have come from India for my sister Nisha-ben's
wedding. There is so much to do. Even I have a job!

"Sona," my grandmother says. "Will you be in charge of stealing the groom's shoes?"

"Why would I do that, Dadima?" I ask.

"It's a tradition for the bride's sister," she tells me. "It's a way for our families to get to know each other."

"I already know Anil-ji," I say, "and what will I do with his shoes, anyway?"

My cousin Vishal sprinkles a handful of petals on my head. "It's like a fun game," he says. "You figure out a way to steal his shoes and then he has to bargain with you to get them back."

I shoo him away.

"Anil's brother will be guarding his shoes," Nisha-ben says. "You'll have to trick Jitu."

"I'll do it!" I say. But I'm not sure.

I've only met Jitu once. I hope I recognize him. "Will Anil-ji and Jitu be here to get their hands painted?"

"Only girls apply *mehndi*," Vishal snorts. "Don't you know anything?"

I stay quiet.

"Did Anil-ji get a white horse to ride?" Vishal asks.

"Of course," Nisha-ben replies.

"A horse!" I gasp. "Do you get to ride one too, Nisha-ben?"

"Only the groom does, *na*?" Vishal gallops around the room. "That's how he gets to the wedding."

Even though Vishal is younger than me,
he thinks he knows everything. He's been to
lots of weddings, but this is my first one.
It's not fair.

That afternoon, Dadima shows me how to mix turmeric, rose water, and chickpea flour into a creamy paste. We rub it on Nisha-ben before she showers. It gives her skin a silvery shimmer, a silky softness, and a fragrant smell.

Later, we hang the garlands
we made over the doorways. We
have created beautiful *rangoli*
designs on the floor with colored
sand. More relatives arrive,
turning our house into a festival.

Vishal keeps babbling, babbling,
babbling. He's such a know-it-all.
I keep plotting, plotting, plotting.
How can I steal Anil-ji's shoes?

Could I dress up as a
robber and snatch them?

Or dump red *kumkum* powder on Jitu to distract him?

Then I have an idea.
But I will need an assistant.

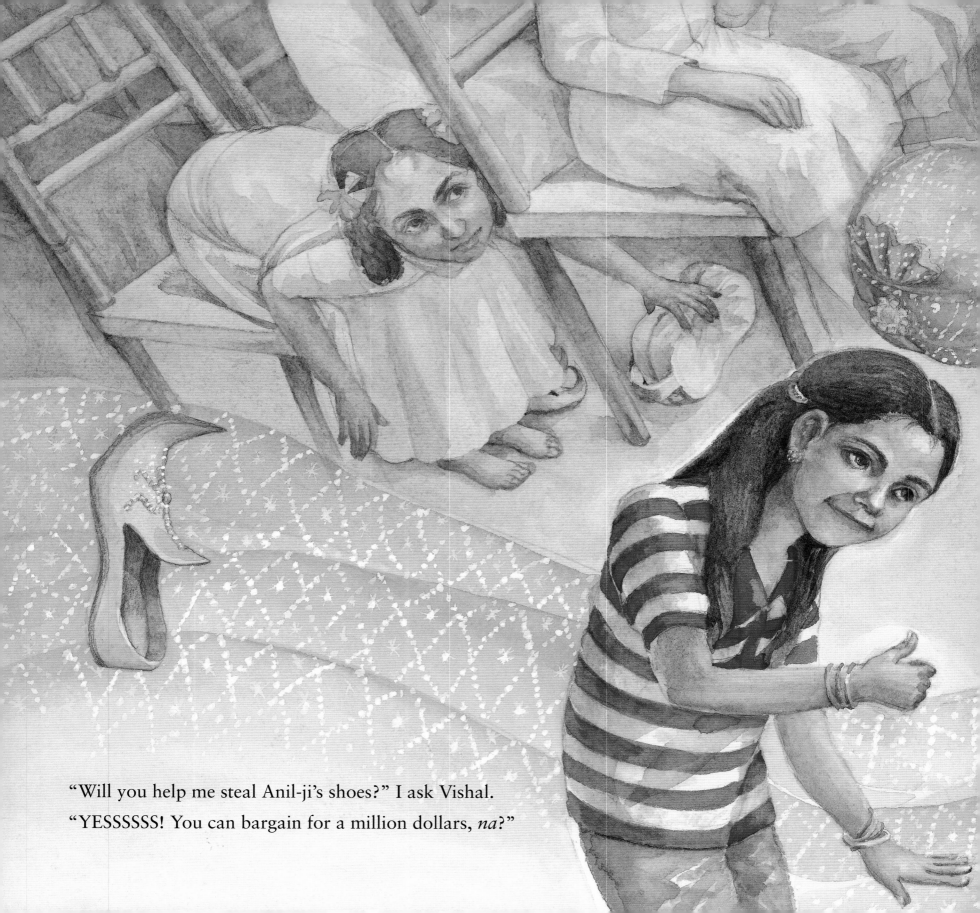

"Will you help me steal Anil-ji's shoes?" I ask Vishal.

"YESSSSSS! You can bargain for a million dollars, *na*?"

"Let's steal the shoes first," I say.
"Then I'll worry about the bargain."
I tell him my plan.

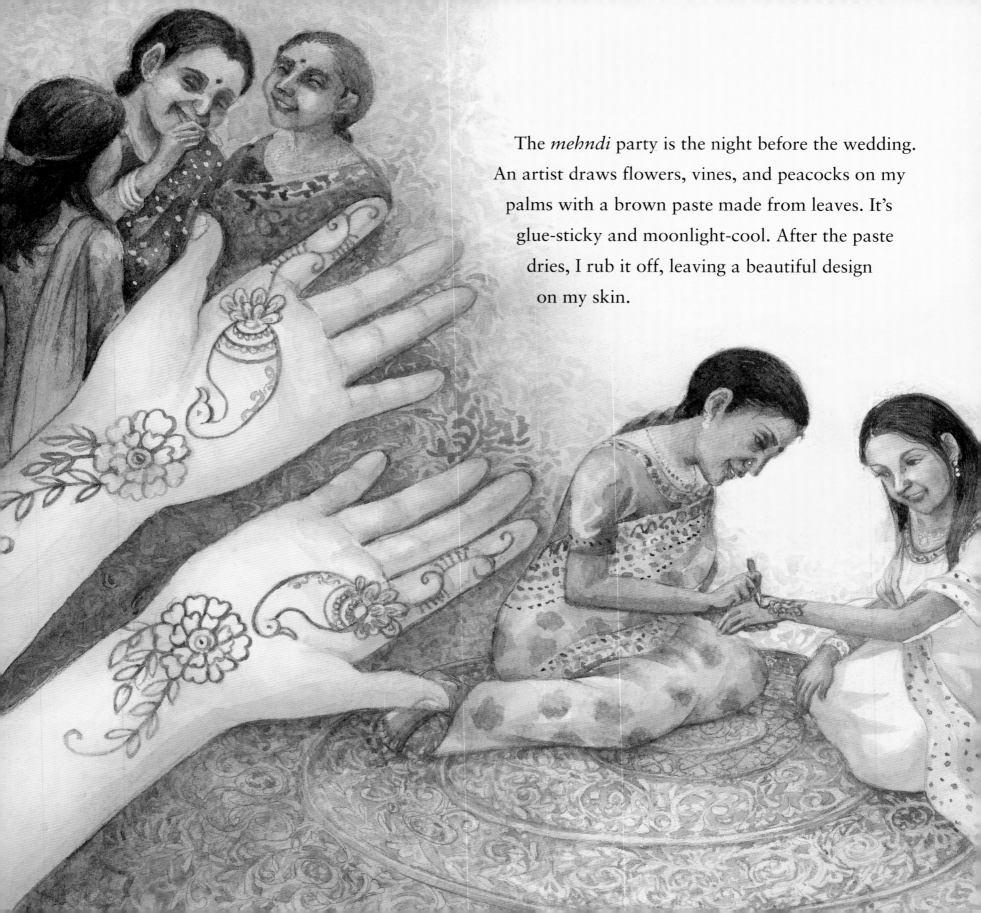

The *mehndi* party is the night before the wedding. An artist draws flowers, vines, and peacocks on my palms with a brown paste made from leaves. It's glue-sticky and moonlight-cool. After the paste dries, I rub it off, leaving a beautiful design on my skin.

The next morning, Dadima fancy braids my hair.

"All set for shoe stealing?" she asks.

"Yes," I say.

But I am worried.

Finally it is time for the wedding. Anil-ji arrives on a
white horse, just like Vishal said. His family and friends dance
around him. The silver threads of his turban shine like stars.

    The horse is handsome, with large eyes and a calm face.
He seems to smile at me. I want to throw my arms around him.

Mom puts a *tilak* of *kumkum* on Anil-ji's forehead for good luck.

Before Anil-ji enters the wedding *mandap*, he takes off his shoes and passes them to his brother. Jitu slips them into a bag, then sits in the front row, just in front of me and next to Vishal. Perfect! He slides the shoe bag under his chair.

"Sona, don't even think about stealing the shoes," he says, as if he knows what I am planning.

"Why would I want Anil-ji's shoes?" I try to look confused.

Nisha-ben is dazzling in her red-gold sari.
For a minute, I forget to breathe.
The priest's voice is loud and soothing,
but I don't understand what he's saying.

"The first thing they do is pray to
Lord Ganesh," Vishal whispers. "Then
they invite the whole universe to the wedding."

"Are you sure?"

"Yes—they invite rivers and mountains,
planets and stars, sun and moon. You don't
understand because it's all in Sanskrit."

It's time. It feels like thousands of flower petals are whirling in my stomach. I nudge Vishal.

"Do you want to wear my turban?" he whispers to Jitu.

"It won't fit."

"It might, *na*? Try it." Vishal tries to put his turban on Jitu.

My heart thumps as I slide the bag out from under Jitu's chair. I remove Anil-ji's shoes, hide them under my long skirt, and put my shoes into the bag instead.

Vishal pushes the turban at Jitu, but it falls into the aisle. Jitu reaches out to grab it and his chair tips over with a clankety-clank. Everyone glares at him.

I collapse back into my chair. No one noticed me!

The priest ties Anil-ji's scarf to Nisha-ben's sari and
they circle the sacred fire several times. First Nisha-ben
leads, then Anil-ji.

"Now they make seven promises," Vishal says.

"What kind?" Jitu asks. I want to know too.

"To not fight, share everything, not keep secrets,
be best friends, and love and stuff like that. Then
they're married."

Nisha-ben and Anil-ji walk out from under the *mandap*.

Dadima and Dadaji are the first to bless them, but then others follow.

Jitu hands Anil-ji the bag. "I kept your shoes safe."

Anil-ji pulls out my shoes. "These are a little too small for me."

Everyone laughs.

"Maybe these will fit?" I hold up Anil-ji's shoes.

"But…but how…?" Jitu sputters. "When did you steal them?"

"Sona, how about if we swap shoes?" Anil-ji asks.

"No way!" I say. "I want a better reward than that."

"What if I give you this turban?"

"No way!" Vishal says. "Sona doesn't need a turban and
I already have one, *na*?"

"He helped me," I explain. "And I already know what I want."

Anil-ji laughs when I whisper my request in his ear, but he agrees.

"Perfect shoe-stealing job," Dadima says.

"That was fun!" I say. "Now I'm ready for my prize."

Author's Note

THOUGH I HAVE ATTENDED MANY WEDDINGS, this story was inspired by my daughter Rupa and her husband Joey. When we were looking at the photos after their ceremony, it became obvious that a picture book about an Indian wedding would be delightful. As I worked on this project, I vividly recalled two other weddings from my childhood and I tried to weave elements from them into Sona's story.

When I was four years old my aunt got married. From the second story balcony of my grandparents' house, I could see the wedding canopy, the crowd milling about the front courtyard, and the roses my aunt tended so lovingly, which were in full bloom. I could hear conversations, laughter, and music. The air was filled with the scents of jasmine and warm milk flavored with pistachio and saffron.

Because my great-grandfather was the adviser to the king of Bhavnagar, I also attended the wedding of the princess of Bhavnagar to a prince from Panna when I was seven. As we waited on the palace grounds, the young groom galloped in on a white horse. His silk attire was embroidered with gold thread and he wore a necklace of square emeralds, each the size of a postage stamp. I was disappointed that I couldn't see the Princess' face, which was covered with her sari, in keeping with the royal tradition. Her arms were filled with gold bangles and she wore gold anklets. This meant that she was from a royal family; only royalty could wear gold on their feet.

Despite attending many weddings, I have never stolen the groom's shoes. This is usually the responsibility of one of the bride's younger siblings. Unfortunately, unlike Sona, I don't have older siblings. At Rupa's wedding, Joey took off his shoes before he entered the area under the *mandap*—the wedding canopy. This is considered a sacred space and no shoes are allowed. That made it easy for my younger daughter, Neha, to steal his shoes and she had fun bargaining with him after the ceremony! She was happy to exchange his shoes for the book Joey had wrapped up for her.

THE WEDDING DEPICTED in this book is a Hindu ceremony. Hinduism is the major religion practiced in India. Weddings are usually conducted in the Sanskrit language and can last a long time—sometimes hours and hours. They may include many different rituals; some of the important ones are described in this book.

India is a very large country, and wedding traditions vary from one region to another. Shoe-stealing, for instance, is only done in some parts of the country. Many Indian-American families, like Sona's, continue to practice traditions like this, which come from their home regions.

Not all grooms arrive on horseback, as Anil does. Some ride in cars or horse-drawn buggies, and others walk. Occasionally, a groom might arrive on an elephant!

A wedding represents the merging of two families, and many of the traditions are intended to communicate that to the members of the wedding party and the guests. Sona and Nisha's mother applies a *tilak* of *kumkum*— a religious mark made of saffron or turmeric dissolved in lime to make it red—to Anil's forehead to welcome him to the family and wish him good luck. At the end of the ceremony, the newly married couple receives blessings from their elders—grandparents, parents, and other important members of their family and the community. Now they are ready to start their married life.